NICK WOULD grew up in Lincolnshire, and took a combined degree in English, Philosophy, American Literature and Ancient History at the University of Leicester. After three years of teaching, he moved to London to write song lyrics and children's stories. In 1992 his song 'Greyclouds' was chosen by the elephant charity Elefriends as its flagship song, released on disc and nominated for an environmental award. He collaborated with the artist Brian Grimwood on *Grimwoods Tails* (Elfande), a collection of rhyming stories accompanied by a cassette of Nick's music. His latest work is the Dawn Walkers trilogy. Nick is married to textile designer Maggi Waud and lives in Crouch End, London.

EVIE SAFAREWICZ trained as a ceramic designer before becoming a freelance illustrator. She is an enthusiastic traveller, taking a particular interest in the peoples and landscapes of Africa. Her previous books include *Steaming Cook Book* (Collins), *Bouquet de Provence* (Pavilion), *A Proper Breakfast* (Johnson Editions) and most recently, *Grandma's Garden* (Dorling Kindersley) and *The King Who Wanted to Touch the Moon* (Ginn & Co.). Her first book for Frances Lincoln was *Chinye*, a West African folk tale retold by Obi Onyefulu.

SERENGETI PLAIN

oL DoINyo LE NKAI

NGoRoNGoRo CRATER

RIFT VALLEY

NORTHERN

ABOUT THE MAASAI

The Maasai are a nomadic tribe found in Kenya and Tanzania who herd their cattle in the area stretching from Mt Kilimanjaro through the Maasai Mara Game Reserve down to Lake Turkana. They speak the Kimaasai language. The southern Maasai are divided into several geographical areas, each with its own clan, including *Purko, Loita, il-keekoonyokie, il-moitanik, il-damat, il-wuasi-Nkishu, I-sambur and i–siria.*

The Maasai keep close spiritual links to the natural world about them and retain their age-old customs. Boys go through several well-defined rites of passage; after initiation they become warriors, living with their mothers and sisters until they are about 30, when they can marry and become elders. Girls usually have marriages arranged for them by their fathers, and older women hold the same highly-respected status as male elders.

Like all African tribes, the Maasai have been greatly affected by modern civilisation. Vast tracts of land have been taken away from them to make way for national parks. The introduction of farming, which limits the free movement of livestock, has made other people richer but the Maasai poorer. They are now trying hard to adapt to modern technology and enter the economic mainstream. But despite these changes, they continue to be the dignified, proud and unique people they have always been.

GLOSSARY

boma – Maasai settlement surrounded by a hedge

moran – junior warriors

panga – long-bladed knife

manyatta – junior warriors' settlement

The Warrior and the Moon copyright © Frances Lincoln Limited 2001
Text copyright ©Nick Would 2001
Illustrations copyright © Evie Safarewicz 2001

With thanks to Grace Mesopirr-Sicard, consultant on the Maasai
and author of *A Tale of a Maasai Girl* (BG)

First published in Great Britain in 2001 by
Frances Lincoln Limited, 4 Torriano Mews
Torriano Avenue, London NW5 2RZ

First paperback edition 2002

ISBN hardback 0-7112-1486-7
ISBN paperback 0-7112-1487-5

Set in Sabon

THE WARRIOR AND THE MOON

SPIRIT OF THE MAASAI

❋

Nick Would
Illustrated by Evie Safarewicz

CONTENTS

❋

FRANCES LINCOLN

SPIRIT OF THE MAASAI

No one forgets their first glimpse of a Maasai warrior.

Mine was in 1989, when I visited Tanzania for the first time to stay with a friend in Moshi. We were driving up through the Ngorongoro highlands on our way to the crater. The land-rover swung round a tight corner – a sudden flash of sunlight on spear, vivid red cloth, a face of savage beauty, intense eyes, high cheekbones, an aura of such force that I literally jumped back in my seat.

In a second he had vanished. I blinked. "What – who was that?" I asked. And from my friend I learnt for the first time of the Maasai.

When Europeans first encountered the Maasai, they became so enamoured of them that a new word was coined: 'Maasai-itis'. I caught it there and then. What were these fearsome warriors – who would challenge a lion with their bare hands, who could run like the wind, who were kings of their world – what were they really like?

I returned to Tanzania again and again, making long safaris with my friend, climbing Kilimanjaro, observing where I could the ways of the Maasai. And then, finally, I had my chance – a 100-mile walk through the heart of Maasai territory, where few but Maasai ever go, to their Mountain of God, Ol-Doinyo Le Nkai, and then on to Lake Natron. Sixteen Maasai warriors were to be our guards. We would camp under the stars, walk with them, live with them.

That was the most amazing time of my life – staying up through the African night, sitting around a roaring fire, listening to Maasai voices raised in powerful, rhythmic chants. I got to see through their eyes, uncluttered, untainted. Their infectious, bubbling spring of energy and fun filled me and lifted me up. We became friends.

On my return to England, finding it difficult to readjust to London life, I picked up my pen. Stories flowed, woven around these incredible human beings. I hope whoever reads the stories will be inspired, as I was, by the unique, magical spirit of the Maasai.

THE WARRIOR AND THE MOON

The moon shone down on the snows of Kilimanjaro and the surrounding plains. Above, like a million diamonds, the stars sparkled.

In the Maasai boma at Kisongo the children were asleep. But not the *moran*, the warriors. They stood like statues around the *boma* hedge, tall, silent figures in the night, guarding the cattle. Their silver spears glinted in the moonlight. Their eyes searched the darkness. Their ears strained for the slightest sound.

The tallest warrior, Muate, heard something rustle far away in the grass. He raised his spear and moved forward. Under a big acacia tree, by the light of the full moon, he saw lion prints: one male lion, a very big one.

He followed the pawprints further and further into the bush. Suddenly they vanished. It was as if the lion had leapt into thin air and flown away.

Muate shrugged. The lion had gone, that was all that mattered. The cattle were safe.

He turned and looked up into the night sky. As he watched, a big black cloud drifted in front of the moon, hiding it from view. Muate waited for it to pass, waited for the moonlight. But when the cloud moved on, the moon had gone, vanished! Only stars lit the plains below.

Muate ran all the way back to the boma.

The other warriors came to meet him. "Where have you been?" they asked. "Something terrible has happened. The moon has gone."

"Yes," said Muate. "I know. I saw it with my own eyes."

The next morning there was a meeting of the elders. The head man, Ol Oiboni, had a pile of stones in front of him.

"The moon has been stolen," he said. "Muate saw a cloud carry it away. Without the moon's light, our cattle are in danger. The animals of the night will become invisible. We must find the moon and return it to its place in the night sky. I shall cast the stones." He picked up the six stones and let them tumble from his hands to the ground. Then he looked at them very closely.

"What do they say, Ol Oiboni?" asked one of the elders.

"They say, 'The last person to see the moon shall be the first person to see it again.'"

"Muate!" cried the elders as one.

Muate was brought before the meeting.

"The stones have spoken," said Ol Oiboni. "You have been chosen to find the moon."

"When must I leave?" asked Muate.

"When your heart tells you."

—◇◆◇—

Muate sat alone outside his hut, his spear sticking in the ground beside him. This was a task like no other and he did not know where to begin. Yes, he could find a lion, follow its tracks, smell it on the wind. But where could he even begin to look for the moon?

The sun sank, and still Muate did not move. The stars came out. He searched the skies – still no moon. Then his eyes fell upon the dark outline of the mountain, Ol–Doinyo Le Nkai, the mountain of Enkai, God of the Maasai.

When Enkai was angry, smoke would billow from his mouth, and it was said by those few who had climbed to the top that you could hear the voice of God up there, rumbling under your feet.

Muate knew at once what he must do. He must climb the mountain. From there he would be able to see all the heavens, and up there he would listen for the voice of Enkai. Perhaps Enkai would tell him where to find the moon.

—◇◆◇—

It took Muate three days to reach the foot of the mountain. It was evening as he stood in its shadow, looking up the steep grey slopes to the white, crusted top.

"Enkai, I am coming!" he shouted out into the night, and he began to climb. Many times he slipped and fell. The air around him turned cold, and a strange smell seemed to fill the air. Higher and higher he climbed. Soon he would be amongst the stars themselves.

Not until the first rays of sunrise turned the sky pink around him, did he reach the top. He stood on the rim and looked down into the crater below. He saw smoke rising and a pale light coming from cracks in the ground. The smell was very strong now. It smelt like the beginnings of the earth. He pulled his red cloak close around him, gripped his spear and went down into the crater.

The fumes made him feel light-headed. He sat in the shadow of a large rock. The night's climb had exhausted him. His head fell forward. He slept.

Whilst he slept he had a dream.

He dreamt of a huge male lion. It was night and he was chasing the lion. He was about to catch up with the beast when suddenly it changed into a giant bird which flew up into the sky. He watched as the bird climbed ever closer to the moon. Then the monstrous bird opened its beak and swallowed the moon whole. A deep darkness fell, but Muate could still see the bird flying away, towards Ol–Doinyo Le Nkai. As the bird reached the peak, the mountain began to tremble and fire ran down its sides. The bird, in fear, opened its huge beak and the moon fell tumbling down into the mouth of the mountain.

Muate woke up. It was hot, his head felt dizzy. Somehow he knew he must get off the mountain as soon as possible. With weary legs, he clambered up out of the crater and began the long climb down.

Six days after he had left the boma in Kisongo, at nightfall, Muate returned. His people gathered around him.

"Bring him food and water," said the elders. When Muate was rested and refreshed, he stood once more before the council.

"What news, brave warrior?" asked Ol Oiboni. "Did you find the moon?"

"I know where it is."

"Where?"

"It is in the stomach of Ol–Doinyo Le Nkai. The mountain has eaten it."

Ol Oiboni nodded. "Muate speaks the truth, for every night this last week I have seen lights at the top of the mountain."

"But how do we get the moon back?" asked an elder.

Before any could answer, there was a great rumbling. The earth beneath their feet shook.

All eyes turned to the mountain. Thick white smoke was billowing out. There was a deafening crash and a jet of yellow white fire sprang high into the night. They stood and watched as it raged and roared, lighting up the plains below as if it were daylight. Then it began to quieten and fall away, until silence fell and all that remained was a spiral of smoke stretching up into the moonlight – THE MOONLIGHT!

"Look!" shouted Muate. "The moon! The mountain has returned the moon to the sky!"

And everyone started to cheer and dance.

———————— ◉ ————————

NASIRA AND THE WHITE ELEPHANT

Sinyet and her daughter Nasira left the boma as the sun began its descent from the heavens. Each held in her hand a long-bladed knife, a *panga*. They were going to cut wood for the fire. Fire was at the heart of their lives. Its dancing flames kept the beasts of prey away at night, and over its heat they cooked their meals.

Nasira sang as she walked. A breeze billowed her blue cloak. They walked towards a far-off cluster of acacia trees. In the salmon skies above the trees, three vultures circled menacingly.

"Look," Sinyet said, pointing with the blade of her knife, "an animal is in danger. We must go with care."

"Should we not turn back, Mother?" asked Nasira.

"We cannot go back without wood. Let us see what has taken place."

Their footsteps made no sound as they neared the trees. A trumpet scream, high-pitched, fear-filled, split the air.

"Elephant," said Sinyet. "Baby elephant."

They ran forward. The hanging vultures swooped lower. Before them, under the shadowing trees, six hyenas, their teeth bared, encircled a baby elephant. Terror flamed in its eyes. The two Maasai stopped in their tracks. They had never seen an elephant like this before. It was pure white.

"This is the hand of Enkai," Sinyet whispered. Enkai was the Maasai God. All things unusual were the work of Enkai.

The biggest hyena, snarling, leapt at the elephant and sank its teeth into its right ear.

Something stirred inside Nasira. She raised her panga and without thinking ran towards them, screaming at the top of her voice.

"Come back!" her mother cried, but to no avail. She watched, amazed, as Nasira charged, scattering the hyenas like leaves in the wind. They fled before her, scalded by her steaming rage.

The baby elephant stood motionless, blood trickling from its ear. Nasira turned and spoke to it softly, gently. It came to her and she stroked its brow.

Sinyet approached. "Daughter, that was very dangerous, but very brave. I am proud of you."

"Can we not dress its wound? See how its ear is torn."

"Nasira, this is no ordinary elephant. It is white, and so it must belong to Enkai."

"But why is it here on earth, then, Mother?"

"Perhaps it has fallen from the heavens."

"Then until it returns, I shall look after it."

She stood before the young elephant. "We will cut our wood and leave, but I shall return with something for your wound."

And the elephant bowed its head, as if it understood.

Even though the dusk was gathering, Nasira made the journey back to the acacia grove, bearing a gourd of water and some healing leaves. The baby white elephant was still there. Nasira crushed the leaves into the water and bathed its wound. All the time she spoke softly to the tiny calf, soothing and reassuring it. When she was done, she knelt beside it and placed her forehead against its wrinkly trunk.

"If you really are from Enkai, He will come for you. But I shall come again tomorrow, and the day after that, and every day, until you return to your home in the skies."

She stood up, knowing it was time to leave. But before she took her first step, the elephant stretched out its soft white trunk and touched her on the brow, as if bestowing a kiss.

As the last rays of the sun turned the sky flamingo pink, Nasira walked back to the boma.

At first light the next day, Nasira returned to the acacia trees. She carried more water and more healing leaves. But the grove was deserted, the baby elephant gone.

In her heart she was both sad and happy – sad, because she could no longer care for the young thing, and happy, because now it was safely home in the skies with Enkai.

-◈◈◈-

Years fell upon years. The rains came, the dry seasons followed. Nasira grew into a woman. She married and had children of her own At night she would tell them the story of the white baby elephant, and they would fall asleep dreaming of such a wondrous sight.

Nasira's children grew. Her eldest son, Kinai, when he was fifteen, became a junior warrior. He and all his warrior group moved away and made a new boma for themselves, a *manyatta*. And as is the Maasai custom, they took thcir mothers to their new home.

One evening, Nasira sat by the fire. Kinai sat by her side.

"Mother, do you remember the story you used to tell us when we were children – the story of the white baby elephant?"

"Of course, Kinai."

"Was it really true?"

"As true as my name is Nasira."

-◇◇◇-

Three full moons passed. Then came bad news. Nasira's daughter, Simayia, who had remained in the old boma with her grandmother, had fallen ill with the sleeping sickness. Her hands were cold; her forehead was on fire.

Nasira called Kinai to her.

"My son, I must return to Simayia. She needs me."

Kinai nodded. "I will go with you to guide and protect you, for it is a two-day walk. One night must be spent under the stars."

"So be it," said Nasira.

They set off at dawn, Kinai in his red cloak, carrying his spear, and Nasira wrapped in blue. The day was long, the sun hot. Kinai walked at a steady pace, not wishing to tire his mother.

When evening fell, they had covered thirty miles.

"We will make our camp here under this baobab tree," said Kinai. "I shall cut wood and build us a fire."

Nasira sat down and rested her back against the mighty trunk. She could feel the miles in her legs

Kinai heard distant thunder. He looked up. Across the sky a dark cloud was looming. A storm. Why now? he thought, fearing for his mother's comfort.

"There will be much rain soon," Nasira said. "We must build a shelter. I will go and cut wood."

She set off. She had only gone six paces when the heavens were lit by a dazzling bolt of lightning. A deep growl of thunder rumbled across the night. And then came a second flash, so bright that it blinded them for a second. A jagged tongue of white fire leapt down to earth and struck the baobab tree.

Kinai heard a sizzling crack, smelled singed wood. He heard a deafening crash, and his mother called out.

He blinked, not believing his eyes. The baobab tree had split in two. Onc half still stood, smoking from the heat of the lightning. The other half lay on the ground. Beneath it, trapped, lay Nasira.

Kinai rushed to her side. The massive trunk lay across her legs.

"Mother, are you all right? Speak to me!"

She moaned. "Kinai, my legs. I can't move them."

Wildly the young warrior looked around him. What could he do? Rain began to fall, washing his mother's face. He ran to the end of the trunk and put his hands beneath it. Straining every muscle, he tried to lift his mother's burden. It was beyond his strength. Yet he had to move the tree. He had to free his mother.

He looked up into the heavens, the rain beating into his eyes.

"Enkai," he called, "can you hear? Help me! Send me your strength."

The rain stopped and the moon showed its face. The glade was flooded in a pale light. Kinai could see his mother lying under the weight of the stricken tree.

Then the air seemed to move and the ground trembled. Kinai sensed the approach of a giant. He turned, and gasped. In the moonlight – a sight that made his skin prickle – a huge bull elephant as white as the moon towered over him. Its ivory tusks were thicker than a man's body, longer than two spears.

With slow tread it walked to the fallen trunk. Nasira opened her eyes. They filled with wonder.

"You have come back," she whispered.

The giant elephant stooped its head and curled its

trunk around the tree. Kinai rushed to his mother's side and took her in his arms. There was a groaning, a creaking. Slowly but surely the tree lifted. Kinai pulled his mother free. The elephant waited, holding the tree aloft, then slowly lowered it back to the ground.

Softly it trod to where Nasira now lay. Kinai watched as its soft white trunk reached out and touched his mother on her brow, as if bestowing a kiss.

———— ✦ ————

THE ROAD OF STARS

Simpiri looked up at the sun, shielding his eyes. Ah, the sun was so bright today! He checked around him, counting the goats in his small herd, recognising each one. To lose one would be a disgrace for a Maasai boy. Some day, when he was a junior elder, he would have his own herd of cattle. How proud he would be then, how rich!

He gazed across the shrub-land to the giant baobab tree, its twisted arms stark against the African sky. Sitting against its mighty trunk, gazing into the far distance, was Karaini.

No one knew exactly how old Karaini was. His hair was grey, his skin as wrinkled as a bull elephant's, but his dark eyes still twinkled and his wisdom was known and respected by all in Kisongo.

Simpiri called out to him.

"Karaini! Do you want to try and catch me?"

The old Maasai leisurely turned his head and smiled.

"If I want to catch you, young Simpiri, I shall use my tongue and not my legs!"

Simpiri laughed. Karaini always had a clever answer. He could still move very quickly if he wanted to, as Simpiri had found out to his cost more than once.

The young boy walked over and lowered his head as a mark of respect. Karaini patted it affectionately.

"It's cool in the shade," said Simpiri, flopping down beside Karaini.

"That is why I am here," the elder explained, "and not chasing you in the hot sun."

Simpiri plucked a blade of fresh green grass and chewed on it. He looked up through the filtering of leaves and blinked.

"Aiee! It hurts to look at the sun," he complained.

"Then do not look at it," said Karaini.

"Do you know everything?" Simpiri asked seriously.

Karaini chuckled. "I know everything I know. Only Enkai knows everything."

"What don't you know?"

"Much."

"Tell me."

"Aiee, boy! You are like a fly that won't go away."

Simpiri looked crestfallen.

"Very well! I will tell you of something that happened long ago, before you were born. Something that no Maasai can explain. It was the time when the rains never came. We warriors had to go further and further with the herds to find grass. Day after day the sun burnt down, the grass withered and many of our cattle died."

23

Simpiri had heard of this time. It held great sadness. For a Maasai to lose cattle was almost like losing one's life.

"I was sitting here, where I am now, asking Enkai for rain, and I saw a weaver bird fly to the baobab and begin to make its nest. My heart beat fast, for in its beak were tufts of long grass, green grass."

Simpiri's eyes widened.

"Where did the bird get them?"

"I don't know. For two days it kept flying away and returning with more grass. If I'd had wings, I would have followed it."

"Then what happened?"

"Enkai finally sent us rain."

The two sat in silence, watching the goats.

A lone ostrich trotted into view and departed at full speed as Simpiri took up the chase. Karaini laughed at the boy's energy and his foolishness. He would never catch the ostrich.

"Come back and look after your goats," he called after him, "or the lions will have a fine dinner!"

-◇◇◇-

It was midnight. The moon was full, her face clear for all to see. The warriors below, guarding the boma, saw it, but not Simpiri. He lay fast asleep, curled up beneath a thick, warm hide.

In his dream he was up there on the Road of Stars, with a herd of over a hundred cattle he'd captured and was bringing back to Kisongo. He looked down. The fires in the boma sparkled far, far below. His face was bathed in moonlight; he could reach out and touch the stars. They turned green and then, suddenly, total darkness descended. No moon, no stars, no light. He began to fall.

He woke, frightened, and sat up. The familiar bleating of the goats

nearby, the breathing of his brothers and sisters, the howl of a jackal in the night, all this he could hear. But he could see nothing. He blinked, rubbed his eyes. Blackness, darkness. Where had the world gone?

Karaini sat with the other elders in the shade of a giant thorn bush. News of Simpiri's sudden blindness had shaken them all. None had travelled this path before.

Telelia, Simpiri's mother, was distraught. She held her son close to her, folded in her blue robe.

"Karaini, what does it mean?" she asked the elder. "Why would Enkai close my boy's eyes?"

Karaini shook his head slowly.

"There is a reason for all Enkai does. Sometimes it is hidden from us."

"But Simpiri has done nothing wrong!" pleaded Telelia.

"It may be a blessing, not a curse," said one of the elders.

Simpiri spoke, softly, as if from another world.

"Is it because I tried to see the sun's face, Karaini?"

"No Simpiri – there is more to this."

"Without my eyes I cannot look after my herd, I cannot become a warrior, I cannot –"

"Hush, my son," comforted Telelia, holding him even closer. She turned to face the elders. "What is to be done? Have you no medicine, no cure?"

Karaini half-closed his eyes, as if trying to see something beyond his vision.

"There is something," he whispered, "long, long ago…"

—o-⊙-o—

It was dawn the following day. Telelia was milking the cows. Karaini came to her.

"Enkai spoke to me in the night."

Telelia stopped her work and looked up. "Simpiri?"

"To find his eyes again, he must return to the place where he lost them."

Telelia shook her head. "But that is impossible. He was in dreams, walking the Road of Stars."

"That is where we must return," Karaini said simply.

"But how?"

"I shall take him above the clouds, to the top of the forested mountain. There we will be in the stars."

Telelia gasped. "The cold place? No one climbs there. It is not a place for Maasai. We are people of the plains. Under the tall mountain trees, they say it is always night."

"Do you wish Simpiri to see again?"

"Yes, of course."

"Then bring him to me after milking."

—o-⊙-o—

Karaini hacked at the thick undergrowth with his panga. Simpiri held on to his cloak, fearful of this new world – its strange smells, its startling noises.

They climbed and climbed until their legs ached. Once, while they rested, the sound of devils broke above their heads, discordant barking and grunting. Simpiri cowered close to Karaini.

"Do not fear," Karaini said. "It is only white-beard monkeys."

They walked up into the clouds, a world of grey mist which enveloped them with icy dew. Karaini shuddered – the mountain was well named.

It took the old man and the young blind boy three days to climb where no man had been before. They made their evening camp between the fluted roots of a huge kapok tree and lit a fire.

Karaini breathed deeply. They were now above the clouds and the air felt thinner. He looked into the heavens. The milky-white Road of Stars was close enough to touch. They had returned to the place of Simpiri's dreams.

Simpiri slept deeply in a world of darkness. Karaini sat by his side, leaning against the kapok tree. The cold seeped into his old bones. He had done his part; they were now in Enkai's hands.

His head nodded forward, sleep overtook him. And as he slept, his soul took flight, beyond the stars. The voice of Enkai whispered into his ears, "The way down leads first to the top."

✦ ✦ ✦

Simpiri woke to the barking of monkeys. The air was crisp and clean, the sky a washed blue – BLUE!

"Karaini! I can see! I can see!" He leapt up and ran around and around, shrieking, whooping. His joy was short-lived, for his new eyes fell on his old friend.

Karaini sat there ashen, changed, shrivelled. His bones ached. He tried to stand, but could not do so without Simpiri's help.

The young boy knew how much he owed to Karaini. If he had had the strength, he would have gladly carried him back down.

"We must leave at once," he said. "It is the cold that hurts you. We will go slowly."

"No!" said Karaini.

"No? But why not?"

"First we must climb to the very top."

Simpiri's eyes widened in disbelief.

"Hear me, boy. Enkai spoke to me in my dreams: *The way down leads first to the top.*"

"But you are weak, Karaini," Simpiri pleaded.

"It is not far. Enkai has a purpose. We must go on."

Karaini was right: it was not far, but it took all morning. He had to lean heavily on Simpiri's shoulder and stop frequently to recover his breath. It tore at the young boy's heart – surely Enkai could not wish such suffering.

The ground rose steeply and stopped. The summit was in sight. Inch by inch they climbed until finally they reached the top.

They looked down – and gasped. A crater, so enormous that the far rim was almost beyond sight, encircled a hidden world far below them. The inside of the mountain had sunk down and lay there, hidden. Their eyes took in forests, a river, a glittering lake rimmed with pink – a whole world, lost and unknown above the clouds.

They saw elephant, vast herds of zebra and wildebeest, grazing on lush pastures of grass – green, green grass!

"This is where the weaver bird came," whispered Karaini.

They sat and rested, drinking in the new world below them. Then they turned, Karaini leaning on Simpiri's shoulder, and began their way back down the mountain.

And that is how the Maasai found Ngorongoro – the Cold Place.

————— ✦ —————

SENDEYO AND THE RAIN GOD

The lands of the Maasai once stretched for ever, from the deserts north of Mount Kenya to the plains south of Mount Kilimanjaro, from the shores of Lake Victoria to the beaches of the Indian Ocean. Over these plains roamed their herds of cattle, goats, and donkeys, grazing on the lush grass. Life had always been this way. The seasons turned, the rains came, the sun rose.

Until now. Not even the great Ol Oiboni could remember a time like this. There had been no rain for many months, not a single drop. Rivers had run dry, water holes were empty. Every day the sun beat down in a baking sky. The grass was parched and yellow. The cattle were thin. If the big rains did not come soon, many would die.

At night, in the boma of Kisongo, around the fire, the elders sat together, staring into the flames. They did not see Sendeyo, son of Muate, listening in the shadows.

Ol Oiboni spoke. "The God of Rain is a giant leopard who lives in the sky. From his eyes the lightning flashes, and when he growls, the thunder rumbles. The Leopard God has gone on a long hunt beyond the stars. There will be no rain until he returns."

"But when will he return? He has been gone eight full moons."

"I have asked the stones many times for this answer, but even they do not know. I will try again."

He took from a leather pouch six white stones and held them in his cupped hands. He kissed them and then tossed them up in to the air. They landed at his feet.

Everyone fell quiet as Ol Oiboni studied them. At last he spoke.

"The stones have something new to say: 'The child that cannot be seen shall see the Leopard God.'"

"What does it mean, Ol Oiboni?"

Ol Oiboni shook his head and continued staring at the stones.

Sendeyo slipped away, unseen.

He returned to his hut. His father Muate was there. The young boy bowed his head for his father to bless him.

"Father," said Sendeyo. "Do you remember you once told me a story of our warriors, long ago, when they went to war? They made themselves invisible so that the enemy could not see them."

Muate smiled. "Yes, I remember the story."

"How did they make themselves invisible? I've forgotten."

"They made a paste from the eggs of the black mamba and smeared it over their bodies."

◦◦◦

Sendeyo couldn't sleep. The stones spoke of a child that could not be seen. He was a child. The eggs of the black mamba snake could make you invisible. That very morning, in the rocks behind the boma, he had discovered a black mamba's nest with twelve white eggs. It must be a sign.

He knew what he had to do, but the black mamba was deadly poisonous. He would have to be very careful.

All the following day Sendeyo waited for his chance. Finally, just before sunset, the black female snake slithered from her hole in the rocks to hunt for food. In a trice Sendeyo was there. He took just three eggs.

He sat at the back of the hut holding a wooden bowl with the eggs in it. With the end of a stick he made a paste with them and began to smear it over his body. When he was finished, he stood up in the moonlight.

"I am invisible," he said. "I shall go seek the Leopard God."

He walked through the dusk, past the fire, past children playing. No one paid him any attention. He came to the hedge that surrounded the boma and passed through the entrance. No one saw him go.

A full moon hung in the sky above. A soft breeze carried the distant howl of hyenas to his ears. He could feel the warmth of the earth under his feet, could smell the dry dust. He walked and walked, scanning the skies for signs of the Leopard Rain God.

-◈-◈-◈-

Muate returned from the fire to his hut. His wife met him, frantic with worry.

"Muate, is Sendeyo with you? I can't find him!"

"No," said Muate. "He was here when I left."

"Where can he have gone?"

And suddenly Muate knew. He stood still and let the thought sink in. He searched the hut. Behind it he found the wooden bowl. He lifted it to his nose and sniffed. "Mamba," was all he said, as he took up his spear and made for the door.

"Where are you going?" asked his wife.

"To find our son."

-◈-◈-◈-

Sendeyo stood at the side of what was once a river. Now it was a dried-up, dark grey valley, snaking away left and right. He clambered down into it.

Footsteps – small human footsteps! The sleepy leopard raised its head. It had not eaten since sunrise. It stirred, sat up and sniffed the air. Silently it crept through the long grass, a shadow in the night.

Sendeyo followed the river bed. Perhaps a river, even a dried-up river, would lead to water.

Suddenly there was a deep rumble close at hand. Was it thunder? Or was it the growl of a big cat? The boy stood still, listening. There was a dazzling flash of light in the sky, snakes' tongues darting down to earth.

And then, in the moonlight, a huge cloud grew above him. It hovered over the plains. Again it rumbled, again it blazed the sky. Sendeyo stood amazed. The Leopard God of Rain had returned!

The hungry cat was now only ten feet away. It crouched, ready to leap.

The lightning flashed, the leopard sprang. Sendeyo saw it out of the corner of his eye and turned, unbelieving.

He was knocked from his feet and sent sprawling to the ground. He landed on his stomach, winded, and looked up. His father Muate was already back on his feet, spear in hand, facing the snarling cat.

A huge crash of thunder rumbled across the heavens. A bolt of lightning lit the two of them, facing each other in icy silence. Then, slowly, the leopard began to back away. Darkness closed around him. He was gone.

Muate and Sendeyo reached the boma at sunrise. The skies above them were heavy with cloud.

Ol Oiboni and the elders met them at the entrance.

"Muate, you have found your son!"

"Yes," replied the warrior. "And my son found the leopard. See for yourselves."

With his spear he pointed to the skies. The heavens opened and the rain fell – a great waterfall.

———— ✺ ————

FOOTPRINTS IN THE WIND

The warrior could not go on much further. His foot felt like fire and was swollen grotesquely. Water, he must drink soon. His gourd was long empty.

With aching eyes he scanned the horizon and then suddenly, there it was: safety, water, shade – the giant baobab. Thirty warriors, arms linked, could not have encircled it. Thousands of years old, but today, here for him. Slowly, painfully, he began to limp forward.

He sensed danger, turned. A huge shadow was thundering towards him. He froze.

The cold fingers of dawn touched and stirred him from his troubled sleep.

Sokai sat up abruptly, breathing heavily. What did this dream mean? Why did it visit him so often?

It was evening in the manyatta at the foot of Ol-Doinyo Le Nkai, the

Maasai's Mountain of God. A fire burnt brightly under the stars. Around it the moran, the junior warriors, were gathered. They were excited. Three lions had been seen at dusk hunting zebra. The Maasai had given chase and driven the lions far from their territory.

All their cattle were now safely inside the thick hedge that surrounded the manyatta, safe from hungry predators, protected by the warriors. They were singing the praises of Sokai. All moran can run like the wind, but Sokai was the fastest and bravest of them all.

A song broke out, a rhythmic, earthy chanting over which one high voice sang the story of the lion chase. When the song was over, Sokai stood up and moved into the firelight. This was a signal for their favourite dance.

Another breathy chant began, faster this time. Sokai took two little jumps into the air and then, defying gravity, leapt effortlessly straight up, over three feet from the ground, trembling his shoulders at the peak of his jump. One by one the other moran took their turn, each trying to outdo the other by leaping higher, but none could out-jump Sokai.

After the singing and the energy of the dance, a peace settled over the manyatta. Sokai gazed up at the Holy Mountain. Trails of fire snaked down its sides, molten rock that Enkai was spitting out from the top. Enkai was angry.

Sokai was about to speak when he sensed movement in the air, heard footprints in the wind. A sudden, violent tremor shook the ground. The moran leapt to their feet, clutching their spears, their eyes searching the darkness. The baying of cattle, the bleating of distressed cattle filled the night. It was as if a massive boulder had dropped from the sky, shaking the earth as it landed.

Swiftly, in silence, the warriors made their way to the outer hedge, ready to meet whatever danger threatened. There was another tremble, then another and another. Like giant footsteps, they continued for several minutes until they began to fade, as the giant moved further away.

Silence returned. The animals grew calmer.

"What beast could make the earth shake like that?" one of the moran asked.

"Not even the biggest bull elephant," replied another.

"This is the work of Enkai," said Sokai. "If it is a beast, it has come from Him and we must go out to meet it."

The night sky began to pale. Sokai watched. It was cold. He kept his warm red cloak wrapped tightly around him.

A rim of molten gold edged over the horizon. His spear flashed with the first rays of dawn light. The shadows of night took flight as the vast African sun heaved itself up into the sky and a new day began. It was time to leave.

It was the custom for warriors to travel in twos – then, if one was hurt, the other could fetch help. But no other warrior could keep pace with Sokai. He chose to go alone. The footprints had come to him in the wind. He would have to travel far, and to catch the wind would take all his famed speed of foot.

He began to run, gazelle-like, further and further, his eyes raking the

horizon, scanning the earth at his feet. He recognised the padded print of lion, the deep orb indent of elephant, the slither of python, but nothing he had not seen before.

At noon he rested, sticking his spear into the ground, blade skywards. From his gourd he drank deeply of cow's milk. He knew from the sun it was time to turn, if he was to be back by night within the safety of the manyatta hedge.

Then he heard them again – footprints in the wind. The ground shuddered.

To his right was a foresting of flame-trees. Their fiery tops began to sway. Whatever Enkai had sent was there amongst the trees. He grabbed his spear from the ground and moved forward.

He crouched within the shadow of the trees, listening, watching. The giant footsteps had ceased, the air was still, all was quiet. Either the mighty beast was aware of the warrior's presence and had frozen, or it had flown into the skies.

Sokai advanced.

At the heart of the flame-trees was a clearing. He glanced down and stopped in disbelief. Like all warriors he knew the footprint of every animal.

He recognised this print well: it was rhino, unmistakable – but there was something very different about this print. It was more than twice the normal size! Such a rhino would be as tall as a giraffe, as wide as a baobab, its power awesome. But where could such a huge animal hide? Only moments ago it was amongst these trees, and now it was no more.

Sokai prodded the rhino prints with his spear. The sheer weight of the beast was obvious from their depth.

He moved on down to a ravine. At the water's edge the prints ran out.

Sokai's instinct told him to return to the manyatta, but another voice kept saying, "Go on". What should he do? He would sit and think in the shade of the trees.

Perhaps his uncertain state made him, for once, careless. He spotted a large stone to sit on, went to pick it up and carry it to a nearby trunk. Beneath such stones lurked danger. He saw it too late. As his hands raised the rock into the air, the scorpion darted out on the attack. Its tail arched over, piercing Sokai's heel, injecting its poison deep into him.

He yelped, dropping the rock. He knew at once his folly, at once the consequences.

–◊◊◊–

The sun was beginning to set. The warriors had returned, all save Sokai. Their searches had been fruitless; the huge beast had left no tracks. Truly it must have come from Enkai. But the invisible beast was not their main concern.

"I should have gone with him," said Masiani. "Why has he not returned?"

"He will return. Sokai will not be caught."

But none were comforted. These were strange times. The warriors' hearts told them their brother was in danger. Masiani spoke again.

"At first light tomorrow we will set out. His tracks will lead us to him."
And so it was agreed.

-◇-◇-◇-

The sun woke Sokai, lying beneath an acacia tree. He ached all over. He tried to move, and winced..

His foot raged. Looking down, he saw how badly it had swollen overnight. Walking today was going to need all his courage. Leaning heavily on his spear, he managed to stand. His poisoned foot throbbed, felt like fire. He tried to hop on his good one. It was agony, but he tried again, and again.

-◇-◇-◇-

Masiani picked up the trail first.
"See here, this is Sokai's tread."
The four warriors set off in full flight. Time was running out.

-◇-◇-◇-

Sokai blinked through the pain. Something was wrong. He didn't recognise this landscape. Surely he could not have lost his way? He reached for his gourd to quench his fevered thirst. It was empty.

He could not go much further. Shade, shelter, water – if he could find these he could rest and wait. His brothers would come and find him.

And then suddenly, there it was, standing alone. Sanctuary: the baobab of his dream, its colossal trunk full of water, its seed-pods full of white nourishing pulp, its writhing arms reaching out to him, beckoning him to come home.

There was a stirring in the air around him. He froze.

Turning slowly, he saw it watching him – a gigantic black rhino, impossible to believe, yet frighteningly real, snorting, squat, ready to charge. It lowered its massive curved tusk.

Sokai knew he had to get to the tree, that his life depended on it. He ran. Fear overcame his pain. He heard thunder, felt the earth shake, knew the rhino was giving chase.

The tree drew ever nearer. Sokai turned. The black shadow was about to engulf him. He could feel the heated breath of the beast on him, saw the evil gleam in its eyes. At the very last moment he threw himself to one side. The rhino charged headlong into the baobab at full speed, sinking its tusk up to the hilt in the broad trunk.

It tried to pull back, but the baobab held fast. Trapped, enraged, the rhino bellowed to the heavens. The two primal forces locked in a titanic struggle. Sokai watched spellbound as the rhino shook and shook the giant tree, wrenching and bulling, trying to wrest itself free. But it had met its match.

The colossal beast gave one last bursting of neck muscles. There was a bone-splintering crack as its tusk, still deeply embedded in the belly of the tree, snapped off at the root. The rhino staggered back, clumsily. Confused, stunned, it howled, then turned and ran.

Sokai lay back, his heart pounding. He gazed up in wonder at the ancient tree. From the wound in its trunk a stream of water, life-giving water trickled. He crawled to it and drank deeply. Then, exhausted, he fell into a deep, deep sleep.

As he slept, the baobab began to stir. On one night, and one night only each year the giant tree blossoms – large, sweet-smelling flowers, white stars against the evening sky. Bats began to circle, drawn by the nectar. Underneath, unaware, Sokai slept on. When the creatures of the night had taken their fill and vanished, the blossoms wilted and fell, covering the sleeping Maasai below with a blanket of faded stars.

⊙ ⊙ ⊙

Two nights and two days passed.

Sokai awoke, not knowing where he was. Masiani's face was grinning down at him.

"You are safe, my brother," he said, "back in your home, in the manyatta."

"You found me!"

"We followed your trail to the acacia tree. Your wound has been tended. It is healing."

"Acacia? But I was at the baobab. Did you not find me there?"

Masiani frowned. "There are no baobabs on those plains – you know that."

"But the rhino ... Were there no footprints?"

"Only yours, my brother."

⊙ ⊙ ⊙

Sokai lay alone, uncertain. Had his fever made him dream? It had all seemed so real. But if it was real, how could they have found him back at the acacia tree? Was this the work of the scorpion's poison?

He reached into his cloak for his gourd, now filled with fresh milk, but his fingers touched something else, something soft and moist. With trembling hand, he brought it to his eyes.

It was a dying star, a fallen blossom from a baobab tree.

⊙⊙

SERENGETI PLAIN

OL DOINYO LE NKAI

NGORONGORO CRATER

NORTHERN RIFT VALLEY

OTHER PICTURE BOOKS IN PAPERBACK FROM FRANCES LINCOLN

CHINYE
Obi Onyefulu
Illustrated by Evie Safarewicz

Poor Chinye! Back and forth through the forest she goes, fetching and carrying for her cruel stepmother. But strange powers are watching over her, and soon her life will be magically transformed... An enchanting retelling of a traditional West African folk tale of goodness, greed and a treasure-house of gold.

Suitable for National Curriculum English – Reading, Key Stages 1 and 2
Scottish Guidelines, English Language – Reading, Level B

ISBN 0-7112-1052-7 £5.99

THE TIME OF THE LION
Caroline Pitcher
Illustrated by Jackie Morris

At night-time, when Joseph hears a Lion's roar, he decides, against his father's advice, to go and meet the Lion. He sleeps beside him, meets his brave lioness and watches the cubs play, learning that danger is not always where you think. Then one day traders come looking for lion cubs...

Suitable for National Curriculum English – Reading, Key Stages 1 and 2
Scottish Guidelines English Language – Reading, Level C

ISBN 0-7112-1338-0 £5.99

THE COMING OF NIGHT
James Riordan
Illustrated by Jenny Stow

When the great river goddess Yemoya sends her daughter Aje to marry a chief in the Land of Shining Day, Aje pines for the dark shadows of her mother's realm. So her husband sends Crocodile and Hippopotamus down to the river to bring back a sackful of Night... A Yoruba creation myth from West Africa that will delight young readers.

Suitable for National Curriculum English – Reading, Key Stages 1 and 2
Scottish Guidelines English Language – Reading, Levels B and C

ISBN 0-7112-1378-X £5.99

Frances Lincoln titles are available from all good bookshops.

Prices are correct at time of publication, but may be subject to change.